Cindy Eller

A Modern-Day Cinderella Tale

SETTINGS

An apartment building and a ball field

Narrator: Once upon a time, in an apartment building in a big city . . .

Mr. Eller: Good morning, Cindy. I hate to leave you with such a mess. But I have to open the store. Saturday is our busy day, princess.

Cindy Eller: It's okay, Dad. You work hard. I'll pitch in. *(to herself)* Wow! Every dish in the kitchen is dirty. And is that oatmeal on the wall?

Narrator: Meanwhile, next door . . .

Mrs. Ferry: We love to have our favorite nephew visit. Another pancake, Perry?

Perry: Thanks, Auntie F. I hear that your company is doing well. I love your ads: "Speedy help for needy folks." Say, it sounds like the Eller family next door is busy as usual.

Mrs. Merry: Honey and Candy must be getting ready for another lesson. Their mother, Meena, is *always* taking them somewhere. Art lessons, music lessons, dance lessons.

Perry: What about their stepsister, the one you both like so much?

Mrs. Ferry: Poor Cindy! She stays home and does all the housework. Her Dad is always working at his store—

Mrs. Merry: —while Meena and her girls play and spend money on themselves. Mrs. F., let's check on Cindy again.

Perry: I'd like to tag along.

Narrator: The neighbors bump into each other in the hallway.

Meena: *(rudely)* Watch out, Mrs. Ferry and Mrs. Merry. Honey! Candy! Let's go! We're late for baseball practice. I'm getting my girls ready for the All-City All-Star tryouts. They're four months away.

Honey: We're already the best players in our *school*.

Candy: Now we'll be the best in the *city*!

Mrs. Ferry: We stopped by to see Cindy.

Meena: Well, don't waste her time. She has to do housework. The rest of us have so many other things to do!

Mrs. Merry: *(whispering)* Oh, please!

Meena, Honey, and **Candy:** We're off!

Narrator: After Meena, Honey, and Candy leave, Mrs. Ferry, Mrs. Merry, and Perry enter the Eller home.

Cindy: Hi, Mrs. F. and Mrs. M. Hi, Perry!

Mrs. Ferry: Did a tornado hit this kitchen? Oh, well. We'll take care of it!

Mrs. Merry: Cindy, why don't you and Perry get some fresh air? Let's get to work, sister!

Narrator: Cindy and Perry go outside on the balcony.

Cindy: You coach a baseball team, don't you?

Perry: Yes, I do. Your sisters are really into baseball. What about you?

Cindy: I like baseball, but I don't get to play much. I have so much work to do. Oh, this isn't fair. Your aunts shouldn't be doing my work. Let's go back inside. *(loudly)* Mrs. F., Mrs. M., let me help ... *(shocked)* Wow! It's all clean!

Mrs. Ferry: We're quick workers, dear! Now, we couldn't help but hear what you said to Perry.

Mrs. Merry: We think you should join a baseball team too, Cindy.

Perry: I'd be happy to help, Cindy. You could practice with my team on Saturday mornings.

Cindy: That would be super! But what about my chores?

Mrs. Ferry and **Mrs. Merry:** We'll take care of them!

Narrator: For the next few months, Cindy secretly practices with Perry's team. She gets very good, too. Finally, the big day for tryouts arrives.

Mr. Eller: Meena! Honey! Candy! Let's go. You don't want to be late. Cindy can come along and watch. I'm sorry she didn't have time to practice, too.

Meena: Here we are! Don't my girls look gorgeous in their darling new outfits?

Honey: We had to fix our hair just right. If we don't *look* our best—

Candy: —we won't *play* our best! And now we're perfect!

Mr. Eller: Where's Cindy?

Meena: Oh, she said she didn't want to go. Besides, she still has chores to do.

Mr. Eller: Maybe she can come by later. Oh, hi, Mrs. Ferry, Mrs. Merry, and Perry.

Mrs. Ferry: Hi, all! Good luck, girls!

Meena, Honey, Candy, and **Mr. Eller:** Bye!

Narrator: After her family leaves, Cindy comes into the room.

Mrs. Merry: Is that what you're wearing to the tryouts? An old T-shirt and torn shorts? That won't do! Sister, let's go next door and see what we can do.

Perry: Ready for the tryouts, Cindy?

Cindy: I'm a little nervous, but I . . . *(shocked)* Wow! You're back already!

Mrs. Ferry: We just whipped up something special for you.

Cindy: A major league uniform!

Mrs. Merry: And these silver sneakers. Now, tuck your hair under this cap so your stepsisters won't recognize you. There!

Cindy: Wow! I look like a star!

Mrs. Ferry: Go and shine. We'll finish your chores.

Perry: See you later. Come on, Cindy, get into the Pumpkin. That's what I call my orange van.

Cindy: I can't believe I'm really going to the tryouts!

Perry: Just relax and enjoy yourself. Your talent will see you through.

Narrator: A few minutes later, Cindy arrives at the ball field.

Cindy: Here I go!

Honey: Who's that new girl?

Candy: She looks like someone I know.

Honey: Wow! She's pretty good.

Meena: She's not as good as my daughters!

Mr. Eller: What are you saying? That girl is great! She can field and hit. Look at how fast she runs!

Honey: She's running so fast that her cap fell off.

Candy: Why, it's Cindy! What is she doing here?

Meena: She should be home, cleaning up!

Mr. Eller: Cindy Eller, is that you?

Cindy: *(scared)* Oh, no! They know it's me. I've got to go! Where's Perry's van?

Perry: Here! Get in, Cindy. Where's your left sneaker?

Cindy: It must have come off when I slid into home plate. Hurry! We've got to get home before everyone else!

Narrator: Perry drives away very fast. They get back to the apartment in a flash. Cindy puts on her work clothes.

Perry: I'm going back to the field to find your sneaker.

Narrator: The orange van pulls out just as the rest of the Ellers return home.

Meena: *(mad)* Cindy! Come here at once!

Candy: What's Cindy doing in her old clothes?

Honey: She's wearing one silver sneaker!

Meena: Cindy, was that you we saw at the tryouts? Answer me!

Mr. Eller: Stop yelling at her, Meena.

Honey and **Candy:** It *was* you at the tryouts, wasn't it?

Cindy: (*sighing*) It was me. I've been practicing baseball with Perry's team.

Mrs. Ferry and **Mrs. Merry:** She's quite good, too.

Meena: Who's been doing your chores?

Narrator: Before Cindy can answer, Perry returns with the missing sneaker.

Perry: (*out of breath*) I've got your other sneaker, Cindy. Put it on and get back in uniform. I have great news! You made the All-Star team!

Mrs. Ferry and **Mrs. Merry:** Yes!

Mr. Eller: I'm proud of you, princess!

Perry: After you get dressed, I'll take you to the first practice.

Honey and **Candy:** What about us?

Perry: You didn't make the team.

Meena: But I spent a ton of money on them!

Mr. Eller: I guess it's Cindy's turn to play ball. You three will have to do her chores, now.

Meena: Chores? Me?

Honey and **Candy:** We don't know how to do chores!

Mr. Eller: Well, it's time you learned.

Cindy: After all, fair's fair!

The End